THREE TALES FROM
SHAKESPEARE

Written by
Martin Waddell

Illustrated by Mark Oldroyd

Contents

MACBETH

THE SMELL OF BLOOD

The smell of blood was in the air of Scotland.

It was a time of greed, a time of fear and hatred, of ruthless treachery and death. Scotland was ruled by a King called Duncan. He was surrounded by warring nobles who rebelled and rose against him trying to seize his throne. Macbeth, the Thane of Glamis, led the King's army against the rebels. The final battle was fought on a bleak Scottish moor as thunder roared and lightning flashed and men killed and killed again.

The crash of the thunder and the evil on the moor summoned three witches, as crooked as the rocks around them. The dark hags rejoiced in the greed of men, in blood and battle, hatred and revenge.

'When shall we three meet again?' cried one.

'When the hurly-burly's done!' the second cackled. 'When the battle's lost and won. Upon the moor …'

'There we'll meet Macbeth!' the third screeched in triumph.

The lightning flashed once more and they were gone, vanished in the blinding light, as though they had never been.

The battle raged on. Where there was death, there was Macbeth, first to the fight, first to the kill. He waded deep in blood, slicing, stabbing, till at last he came face to face with Macdonwald, the rebel leader.

Macdonwald died horribly, screaming for mercy as Macbeth chopped his head off with a battleaxe.

Grabbing the head by its bloodstained hair, Macbeth held it up in triumph.

'The traitor dies!' he yelled.

And so the battle ended … but not the killing. There were still men to be slaughtered, cut down as they tried to yield or run. The brutal victors killed the wounded, then robbed the bloody corpses of all there was to take, leaving them lying on the battlefield to be picked at by the crows.

It made no difference to Macbeth. He'd won.

Blood-spattered and weary, the victorious army trudged home across the moor. Their drums beat for the terrible victory. Thunder roared and lightning flashed over the moor, and suddenly Macbeth and his friend Banquo found themselves alone. A swirl of thick, foul-smelling mist cut them off from the others, shrouding them in darkness.

Then Macbeth heard a sinister voice.

'A drum! A drum! Here comes Macbeth!' it hissed.

Three witches appeared. It seemed to Macbeth that they rose out of the dank earth. Crouching and leering, they barred his way forward.

'If you can speak, speak!' Macbeth cried, reaching for his sword.

The creatures spoke:
'Hail Macbeth, *Thane of Glamis*!'

Thunder rolled!

'Hail Macbeth, *Thane of Cawdor*!'

Lightning flashed!

'Hail Macbeth, *who will be King*!'

The thunder rolled again ... and died
slowly, while Macbeth stood dumbstruck by
their strange prophecies. He was Thane of
Glamis already but ... the words spun round in
his weary brain.

Hail Macbeth, Thane of Cawdor ...?
Hail Macbeth, who will be King ...?

'You speak fine words for Macbeth,' Banquo
cut in. 'Have you any prophecies for me?'

The creatures cackled, laughing, mocking
the two men who stood before them. They
spoke to Banquo:

'Not so great as Macbeth, and yet greater.'

'Not so happy, but yet much happier.'

'You will not be King, but your sons shall be Kings.'

The strange mist swirled again and, as it swirled, the earth seemed to swallow up the witches. One moment they were cackling and grinning at Macbeth and Banquo, and the next they were gone.

'Gone like bubbles in the air!' Banquo whispered, shocked and scared by what he'd seen.

'I wish they had stayed!' muttered Macbeth. 'We could have learned more.'

'You are to become Thane of Cawdor, and then be King! And my sons will be Kings!' Banquo and Macbeth joked about it, but the words had taken root in their minds. Fear and fierce hope burned in their eyes, though each one tried to hide it from the other.

At that moment a messenger came galloping up, with a message from King Duncan.

'Hail, Macbeth, Thane of Cawdor!' he cried.

Macbeth went pale. *Thane of Cawdor* ... the exact words spoken by the witches.

'He lies,' Macbeth muttered to Banquo. 'It can't be so. The Thane of Cawdor lives ...'

'The Thane of Cawdor has betrayed the King, and is sentenced to die,' the messenger told him. 'The King has named you Thane of Cawdor in his place, as a reward for your bravery today.'

'The witches' first promise!' exclaimed Banquo in amazement.

The first promise had come true ... but the witches had promised more for them ... could such things come to be?

Macbeth's throat had gone dry. His head seemed to spin. He blinked, and took a deep breath, trying to get control of himself. He tried, but he didn't succeed. An idea inside his mind was twisting and turning ... he was thinking words that he didn't want to hear himself say ... terrible words that frightened him. Things he could not, should not, would not speak, whispered in his brain.

The King's sons Donalbain and Malcolm were weak. In those dark days Scotland was ruled by sword and axe and ruthlessness. The man crowned King had to be strong and feared by all the others. If Duncan was not there, who else could the quarrelsome nobles choose to be their King, but the man who had led them to victory?

'If Duncan dies ... I could be King,' muttered Macbeth.

The smell of blood was all around him.

Lady Macbeth waited for news at their castle.

If Macbeth had lost the battle, Macdonwald's men would come as surely as the winter comes. They would take the castle, burning, looting, killing the few men Macbeth had left to guard her there. She knew she would be hacked to pieces, her head stuck on a spike at the gatepost.

If he lost ... but if he *won*, she'd share his glory ... who knew where victory might lead them?

And then a man came galloping up to the castle gates.

'The battle's won. I bring a message from Macbeth!' he told her.

She read the letter quickly. It told of the great victory and the strange meeting with the weird sisters on the moor. 'I will be King if Duncan dies,' she read, and the words burned into her mind. Macbeth was now Thane of Cawdor. Part of the prophecy had come true ... why not all of it?

'Duncan must die,' she thought. 'I must help my husband to kill him.'

She was still wondering where and when and how they could kill the King, when another messenger came, with a message from Duncan.

'The King comes to honour brave Macbeth. He'll sleep within these walls tonight.'

The opportunity Lady Macbeth was looking for had come. The King would be in their castle that very night. Now she had to plan Duncan's death and somehow give Macbeth the strength to carry it through. She knew that killing in cold blood would be very different from killing in battle.

She had her plan ready to tell Macbeth when he returned to the castle.

'The King is here for one night only. Make Duncan welcome here. Flatter him. Don't let him see murder in your face!' she warned Macbeth.

Macbeth hesitated, afraid of what she was asking him to do.

'When Duncan dies … you will be King!' she urged him.

So they prepared to welcome Duncan to their castle.

FOUL MURDER

Lady Macbeth welcomed the doomed King and his two sons, Donalbain and Malcolm. She pretended friendship, smiling and laughing and flattering the man they were about to kill.

Macbeth did not play his part so easily. He talked little and thought much, changing his mind again and again. He wanted to be King, but he knew it would be wrong to kill King Duncan.

The King is here as my guest, eating and drinking and enjoying himself in the home of a loyal friend and kinsman. He suspects nothing! How can I betray him and still call myself a man?

Macbeth's thoughts worried him so much that he slipped away from the feast that had been prepared for the King. He went out of the great hall into the shadows of the torch-lit courtyard. He thought no one had seen him go, but Lady Macbeth followed him, reading the doubts in his mind.

'Why are you hiding out here?' she demanded.

'We can't do it!' he told her.

'We must do it,' she replied. 'Why are you so pale? What has become of your ambition? Why are you afraid of what has to be done? If you are to be King, you must do it.'

'What if we should fail?' Macbeth asked anxiously.

'If you keep your nerve, we'll not fail,' she said.

She told him again exactly what they were going to do, to convince him it would work.

'I'll drug Duncan's servants, so they will be no danger,' said Lady Macbeth. 'You'll kill Duncan while he is asleep. You use the servants' daggers, and smear their hands with his royal blood. We'll accuse them of the murder, and who will dare to doubt us?'

Macbeth took courage from her words. He went back to the table and he laughed and joked with his friend, his guest, his King ... the King he was going to kill, to make the witches' promise to him come true. They stayed up feasting and talking most of the night but, at last, when it was almost morning, the King went off to bed.

Macbeth waited in the courtyard until everyone was asleep.

I will be King ran through his head, as he waited for the signal from Lady Macbeth – the soft ringing of a bell. It would tell him that the drugged drinks had worked and that Duncan's servants were asleep.

Macbeth thought he was alone in the courtyard, but he was not. Banquo was worried and wanted to talk to him.

'The witches' promises ...' Banquo began. 'The first came true and yet ...'

'Not now,' Macbeth said, interrupting him before he could finish. 'These are things that we have to talk about later, things that could mean great honour for you. We'll talk, but let me choose the time to do it.'

'I'll listen to what you have to say,' Banquo said, with his eyes fixed on Macbeth. 'But I know where my loyalty lies. I won't do anything to change that, however great this new honour you speak of may be.'

'Later,' Macbeth repeated, dismissing his friend. 'Go to bed. Sleep well.'

Banquo left, but Macbeth stayed where he was. He hid for a long time in the shadows of the courtyard, waiting for the signal, alone and fearful of what he had to do.

I will be King ... I will be King ...

The words kept hammering in his brain.

I will ...

Suddenly, a strange vision glowed in the darkness before him. It was a gruesome sight ... a dagger, dripping blood. Macbeth reached out for it in fear, but when his hand closed on the hilt of the dagger he found himself clutching nothing.

Then he heard the soft tinkling of the bell which told him that the King lay unguarded, with his servants deep in their drugged sleep.

'The time has come,' he swore. 'Duncan goes to heaven or to hell!'

Macbeth killed quickly, ruthlessly, silently. He stabbed the King again and again with the sleeping servants' daggers. Duncan's blood stained the bed and sheets and floor before Macbeth fled from the room, still clutching the daggers.

Lady Macbeth was waiting for him in the courtyard.

'I heard something!' she said. 'Is he ... did you ...?'

'The deed is done!' he told her.

'And no one ...?'

'One of the King's servants cried out in his sleep,' gasped Macbeth. 'I heard him say, "God bless us!", and another said "Amen!", but they did not leave their beds. I tried to say "Amen", but the word stuck in my throat. I've murdered an innocent man in his sleep. I'll sleep no more ... I've murdered sleep ... I ...'

Then Lady Macbeth saw the daggers still clutched in his bloodstained hands.

'Why did you bring these back?' she said angrily. 'The plan was to leave them with Duncan's servants. You must go and smear their hands with Duncan's blood, and wash the bloodstains off your own.'

'I dare not do it,' he sobbed. 'I can't go back in there.'

'I'll do it!' Lady Macbeth said. Taking the daggers, she ran to the murder room. She smeared blood on the hands and faces of the King's servants.

It was one of the King's most loyal followers, Macduff, the Thane of Fife, who discovered the body. He entered the King's room alone.

Duncan lay dead. Streaks of blood were everywhere, marking the bed, the walls, and the bodies of the King's sleeping servants.

'Murder! Murder and treason! The King is murdered!' Macduff shouted the terrible news and wakened everybody in the castle.

Macbeth was first into the room, his sword drawn. He wasted no time.

He attacked the sleeping servants, screaming with anger, slitting open their throats. Then he stood weeping, his great sword dripping with the servants' blood.

'Revenge!' he cried. 'The men who killed my King have died!'

Macbeth had lost control of himself. He was yelling and lamenting ... talking too much.

Lady Macbeth saw suspicion grow in some faces as they watched. She pretended to faint, to draw attention away from Macbeth ... but she was too late. The damage had been done.

Duncan's two sons left the room quickly.

'If we stay here we'll be in danger,' Malcolm told his brother.

'I see daggers in these men's smiles,' Donalbain agreed. 'They've killed our father. We could be next.'

They fled while the nobles were still arguing about what they should do.

Macbeth seized his opportunity. 'Malcolm and Donalbain arranged to have their father murdered. That is why they have fled,' he declared. The word spread quickly.

Not everyone believed Macbeth, but there was no one strong enough to face him with their suspicions. Macbeth was crowned King by the nobles, as the witches had promised he would be.

Macduff, the Thane of Fife, refused to join in the celebrations. He had found Duncan's butchered body and he had his own ideas about what had happened that night.

Macduff would *not* call Macbeth his King.

He rode away, alone, to his castle.

THE GHOST AT THE FEAST

Macbeth was King, but the terrible thing he had done had changed him. He talked wildly to himself, haunted by strange dreams that would not let him sleep. He saw death and danger all around him, treachery and greed in the faces of his nobles. His dreams made him fear everyone and everything … but most of all, he feared the promise the witches had made to Banquo.

You will not be King, but your sons will be Kings.

Macbeth knew that to prevent the prophecy coming true, Banquo must die.

He arranged a great feast in Banquo's honour. Banquo and his son were to ride to it together. Macbeth knew the route they would have to follow to reach the castle and it was all he needed to know. He made his plan. He was King of Scotland, ruthless, strong. He need trust no one now. He'd do what had to be done.

Lady Macbeth saw the change in her husband.

'My mind is full of scorpions,' he muttered.

She was frightened. If he went on muttering darkly, talking to himself, trusting no one, seeing schemes and plots everywhere … someone would suspect. Somehow she had to make him act normally, but he had turned from her, just as he had turned from everybody else.

'What's done is done,' she told him, desperately. 'We give a great feast tonight to honour Banquo. You must start acting normally, or your guests will be even more suspicious than they are already.'

'There's more to be done,' he muttered, avoiding her eyes. 'It's better if you do not know. Come on now, we must get ready to greet our friends … and especially Banquo.'

The castle glowed with light. A great crowd had gathered in the dining hall. The table was covered in steaming dishes, and fine wine flowed. All the nobles were there … and another man, a dark man, with blood on his face, who had slipped secretly into the hall. He stood by the door and nodded at Macbeth.

Macbeth froze for a moment. Then he took the man aside, and they talked softly together. Macbeth's mood seemed to change. A great weight had been lifted from his mind. Banquo was dead … though his son had escaped the murderers Macbeth had sent to kill him. It didn't matter. Banquo's son was no match for Macbeth … he could deal with the son later … Banquo had been the one he feared.

Macbeth turned from the murderer and moved away to greet his guests, laughing and joking again, as he had not done for days.

The deed is done. Banquo is dead. I have nothing to fear now.

'Banquo is not here although he promised that he would come. Still, we must begin the feast!' he called. 'A good health to everybody! Enjoy your meal.'

The guests began to eat and drink.

'Now where is my chair?' Macbeth asked, looking round. 'There's no seat for me.'

'Your chair is here, My Lord,' said someone.

Macbeth turned round …

He saw Banquo's ghost sitting in the chair before him. The horrible vision had blood streaked on its clothes and face. It grinned and grimaced at Macbeth, accusing …

'You dare not say I did it!' Macbeth screamed at the ghost … but nobody else could see what he was seeing. The nobles watched in amazement as their King shouted at the empty chair.

Lady Macbeth thought quickly. She had to stop him screaming, giving everything away. 'He has these attacks. He's had them since he was a child,' she said to the lords. 'It's best not to pay attention to him and then he will be all right.'

She took him to the side of the room, and spoke fiercely to him. 'There's no one in your chair,' she told him, as he shook with fear. 'No one … look … there's no one … just an empty chair.'

Her words of reason calmed Macbeth. He tried to stop shaking, and bring himself back under control. He looked at the chair and it was empty.

'There's no one,' she said again. 'Nothing! You are imagining things like a child, just the way you imagined the dagger. Be a man!'

The hall had fallen silent. Everyone was watching Macbeth, waiting for his explanation.

'I'm … I'm sorry, my friends,' Macbeth said, trying to sound cheerful and in control. 'I had a funny turn but … but I'm all right now. Come, give me some wine and we'll drink a toast. Let's drink a toast to Banquo!'

He raised his glass to drink the toast, looking round the room with a smile and then he screamed, and screamed again.

Banquo's ghost was standing there, accusing him. Hideous and horrible, the ghost's beard and hair were matted with blood, and gaping wounds oozed red all over its body.

'The King is ill. He needs rest. Leave us!' The Queen ordered the nobles out of the room. They left, muttering to each other about what they had seen and heard. The King and Queen stood staring at each other, and the ruined feast upon the table.

'I saw … Banquo,' he said.

'Banquo? But Banquo didn't come. He isn't here,' she told him.

'I saw him … but Banquo's dead … I know he's dead,' Macbeth said.

She saw in his eyes what he had done.

'Dead,' he said. 'Dead … yet he was here.'

Lady Macbeth didn't know what to do. Since the murder of Duncan, her husband had grown stranger and stranger. She felt that she had no strength to cope with his wild moods and his dark thoughts.

'There's more business to be done,' he told Lady Macbeth. 'Macduff wasn't here tonight.'

'What does it matter if Macduff stayed away from our feast?' she asked.

'I sent for him,' said Macbeth. 'He did not come. He has disobeyed me. He plots against me. No one can do that and live.'

Lady Macbeth clung to her husband. She was frightened. He seemed almost mad and out of her control, yet still filled with fear and fierce ambition. He went on talking of treachery and treason against his throne, and the dangers all around him.

'Another death will make no difference!' he told her. 'Macduff must die! The witches will help me. I'll go to them tomorrow!'

SOMETHING WICKED

Macbeth returned to the moor and the dark cave where the witches lived. He could trust the witches. They knew the future. They would tell him about Macduff. They had told him that he would be King ... they could tell him what he needed to know, and perhaps there would be hope for him in what they said ... at least he'd know the worst.

'By the pricking of my thumbs, something wicked this way comes!' a voice hissed in the darkness.

The three crooked figures were waiting for him, around a huge pot that boiled upon their fire.

'Double double, toil and trouble; fire burn and cauldron bubble,' they chanted together.

Snakes and toads and frogs and bats and dogs' tongues were mixed up in the pot. Lizards' legs, adder's sting, rotting fish, dead flesh and bones all bubbled in the brew.

The witches knew what Macbeth had come to ask, and their answers came in awful visions, rising in the stinking smoke that poured out of the pot.

A head came first. The head was dressed for battle, in a warrior's helmet. The cruel eyes glared at Macbeth.

The mouth opened, and the head spoke:
'Beware Macduff!'

The smoke swirled, and the head was gone.

Next came a small child, dripping blood.
'No man born of woman can harm you.'

The third vision was a child who wore a crown and carried a small tree.

'You will never be defeated, till Birnam Wood shall walk before the castle walls of Dunsinane!'

Macbeth's worries vanished. The visions' words reassured him.

No man can harm me.

I'll never be defeated … till trees walk before my castle walls.

Then a fourth vision appeared through the rising smoke. A man dressed in a King's crown and robes appeared before him. One King was followed by another and then another, and another, till eight Kings walked before him in a line of Kings. They looked alike, yet different, as though each King was followed by his son, who then became the father of the son that followed.

Kings, and sons of Kings …

Then one last vision came, mocking
Macbeth. It was the murdered Banquo, hideous
and blood covered. It grinned with triumph,
pointing at the line of Kings. The last King
raised a mirror and in the glass Macbeth saw
the shapes of others yet to come ... the line of
Kings the witches had promised to Banquo.

Then all were gone. No hags, no head, no slaughtered child, no bloodstained, mocking Banquo with his sons, who would be Kings. The smell, the dreadful cackling hags and the fearful visions they had shown him all vanished in a swirl of smoke.

There was still hope, Macbeth reasoned. The visions had said that no man born of woman could harm him ... so why should he fear Macduff? Trees must walk upon their roots to the walls of Dunsinane before any army could defeat him ... and that could never be.

Macduff! He would summon Macduff to him ... and Macduff would die, like Banquo and Duncan before him!

And then word came that Macduff had escaped from his castle, gone to England to plot with Malcolm, Duncan's son.

'Macduff rebels against me! I'll have my revenge!' Macbeth howled at his followers. 'His wife ... his children ... all his family ... all his friends. Cut them! Kill them! Slice them! Break them! Their spilled blood will be a lesson to all those who doubt me!'

So great was his rage that he would let nothing stand in his way. No one could stand against Macbeth and live. Macduff must learn that lesson.

And so blood flowed again from the

witches' words. The halls, the stairs, the rooms of Macduff's castle, the nursery where the children played ... all dripped with blood, by order of Macbeth, the King.

Macduff had arrived in England and had found Malcolm. Duncan's son was unsure about Macduff. Perhaps Macbeth had sent Macduff to trick him ... to lead him back to a ruthless King, who'd killed and killed again. Malcolm was the son of a murdered King, and like Macbeth, he trusted no one. Macduff had been Duncan's loyal friend ... but friends could change sides. If he stayed where he was, under the protection of the English King, Malcolm knew that he was safe. If he returned to Scotland with Macduff, he might die the same bloody death as his father.

'You must be King, for Scotland's sake,' Macduff pleaded with him.

'For Scotland's sake, I should not go!' Malcolm said, watching him carefully. 'Justice, truth, patience, courage, a strong mind. A King should have these things ... and I have not. I am a man who never should be King.'

Macduff did not give up.

'You are your father's son,' he urged. 'Who killed him but Macbeth? You must avenge your father's death. England will lend us ten thousand men to fight Macbeth. Scotland needs you.'

'I might be a worse King than Macbeth,' Malcolm said, trying to put him off. But Macduff wouldn't listen. They argued and argued, but Macduff's loyalty to Scotland and his murdered King came through in the strength of his words ... at long last Malcolm was persuaded.

'I'm convinced,' he told Macduff, reluctantly. 'You are as you say you are and not some spy sent by Macbeth to lead me to my death. You've come here for Scotland's sake. I'll follow where you lead. Together we will avenge my father's death.'

Then the message came of the terrible massacre. Macduff's wife, his little children, all his family and servants, all who ever served him ... all dead, slaughtered in cold blood within the castle walls by Macbeth.

'Grief sharpens our swords!' Malcolm thundered. 'We've had enough talk! We will have action now!'

'Macbeth must die!' swore many of the nobles. They had had enough of Macbeth and his killings.

The rebel army marched for Scotland, to lay siege to Macbeth in his strong castle on the hill of Dunsinane, close to Birnam Wood.

For Scotland's sake, and for revenge.

THE WALKING WOOD

The tide of fortune had turned against Macbeth.

Malcolm's army stormed through Scotland, with the raging Macduff as their leader. They marched, and as they marched many men came to join them, deserting Macbeth. All those whom Macbeth had murdered seemed to whisper in men's minds, accusing him of bloody slaughter. The nobles who had made him King now turned against him. Men who had been too scared to argue when Macbeth was made King now waited for a chance to slip away and join the winning side.

It wasn't just the whispering dead who spoke against Macbeth. Strange tales were heard of Lady Macbeth. She walked in her sleep, and talked of blood that stained her hands and could not be washed off.

'Out, damned spot,' she muttered, washing her hands again and again, although there was no mark on them.

All she had done was for Macbeth ... but the blood and death and the screams of the slaughtered children broke her mind. She had been strong, now she was weak ... her rambling words of guilt were a danger to Macbeth.

'Who would have thought the old man to have had so much blood in him?' she sighed.

'She's ill. She needs doctors,' Macbeth told his advisers. 'They can heal her.'

'Doctors can do nothing for her,' they told him. 'The Lady needs the help that only a priest can give.'

'I cannot think about her now,' he blazed in anger. 'I have to think about Malcolm and Macduff!'

He'd grown wild and despairing as death and defeat closed in around him, and yet Macbeth still clung to the witches' words.

No man born of woman could harm him. He could not be defeated till Birnam Wood walked before the walls of the castle.

The dark walls of Dunsinane were his protection. 'The traitors will die!' he said, trying to raise the spirits of his men. 'Don't bring me stories about the strength of their army. Don't doubt me. I know I cannot be defeated. Those who speak of doubt will pay the price of treachery and hang before my castle walls.'

His words were strong, but he was wild-eyed and angry, out of control again. Now he had no Lady Macbeth to explain away his screams and curses. His men smelt his fear and muttered. The more cautious made their own decisions. Macbeth would be defeated and would die. They had to leave Macbeth, or they'd die with him. And so more men deserted him with each hour that passed.

Macbeth believed fate was on his side. He had the witches' words. He would win, as he had always won before.

And then he heard the sound of women crying from within the castle walls.

'What time is this to cry?' he asked. 'The enemy will soon be here.'

'My Lord, they're grieving for the Queen,' someone said nervously.

'My wife?'

'The Queen, My Lord. The Queen is dead!'

They were frightened to tell him the news ... and yet when he heard it, Macbeth scarcely seemed to notice. His mind was focused on the battle yet to come before the castle walls, the battle for his life and crown.

'I have no time for this. Why did she have to die now?' he muttered.

He was distracted from his grief by a watchman who cried, 'My Lord ... My Lord ... the woods of Birnam walk!'

Macbeth was stunned. It could not be true. Trees cannot walk ... and yet the woods of Birnam had come to Dunsinane.

It was Macduff, with Malcolm's army. They had stripped the branches off the trees from Birnam Wood and carried them above their heads so that Dunsinane's defenders could not see how many marched against them. Now they were advancing on the castle walls, led by Macduff.

'The witches have betrayed me!' raged Macbeth in despair, as the green branches came on and on and on, advancing toward the walls of Dunsinane.

And then ...

No man born of woman can harm me ...

The witches' words came to him, bursting in his brain ... and he trusted them again.

It was no time to crouch within the castle walls. He could not be harmed. He'd win, as he had always won before ... why doubt it?

'Attack! Attack!' he yelled.

The Macbeth of many battles rose again within him. The castle gates were opened, and screaming with anger and desperate bravery, Macbeth led his men out to his last battle.

Sword and axe and dagger, thrusting, stabbing death was all around the walls. Macbeth led the way, as he always did in battle. Brave as a lion now, convinced he could not die, he hacked his way into the army that attacked him.

He killed and killed and killed again, a ruthless man, a cruel King who never could be beaten. His mind was filled with fire and blood and fame.

Then he faced another man, the man who had to come ... Macduff.

The two men faced each other with their swords, breathing hard, filled with the lust of battle ... but something caused Macbeth to stay his sword, the horror of all he'd done to this man and his family.

'I killed your wife and children!' he shouted at Macduff. 'I've killed enough. Don't make me kill you too.'

'Don't plead with me ...' Macduff said angrily. 'I have no words for you. I leave my talking to my sword.'

'If you hold your ground and fight against me you must die,' Macbeth yelled back. 'Don't make me kill you. You have no chance. The fates are on my side. I have the witches' word for it ... no man born of woman can harm me.'

Macduff raised his sword.

'I was not born as others are, but taken from my mother's body before the time for my birth had come!' he told Macbeth. 'And yet I lived ... and live to kill Macbeth, or die!'

They fought ... and Macbeth's head was cut off by Macduff and lifted high to end the battle.

Macbeth's reign was ended as it had begun, in blood and death.

Trees cannot walk ... but Birnam Wood had walked to Dunsinane. No man born could kill Macbeth ... yet Macbeth's head was held by its hair, by a man who never had been born, but taken from his mother's body, and lived to kill Macbeth. In time, Banquo's sons came to the throne of Scotland. Son followed son, in a long line of Kings.

The witches' words had all come true. They'd played on Macbeth's ambition, to trap him. Their false promises had won Macbeth a bloodstained throne, and led him to a cruel death, the prize of his ambition.

So all must die, who put their trust in evil.

ROMEO AND JULIET

A STREET FIGHT

Early one summer morning a long time ago, two families fought on the streets of Verona. It was an old feud, but the heat of the sun quickened their blood and set them at each other's throats. Men yelled and punched each other and daggers flashed.

The Prince of Verona was hauled from his bed.

'The Montagues and the Capulets are fighting again,' his soldiers told him.

'Those stupid old men!' roared the Prince, rubbing the sleep from his eyes.

'It started with some of their servants and then the young men came and joined in. Now Old Montague and Old Capulet are swearing to get out their swords and fight, though their wives are trying to stop them!' his officer said.

'I'll settle this!' swore the Prince, and he summoned his men with their swords.

The Prince's men flooded out into the streets. They soon put an end to the yelling and screaming and punching and kicking, and they forced the two sides apart.

'Who started this?' demanded the Prince.

The Montagues and Capulets stood and glared at each other.

'I was trying to stop our servants fighting!' Benvolio, Old Montague's nephew tried to explain. 'Then that villain Tybalt drew his sword and ...'

'You lying rat!' Tybalt swore. 'The Montagues attacked us.'

'*You* attacked *me*!' Benvolio shouted. 'You know that you did.'

Tybalt reached for his sword, but the Prince's men stopped him.

'Enough!' said the Prince.

Everyone stopped. Everyone had to stop when the Prince spoke. His word was law on the streets of Verona.

The Prince turned to the two old noblemen from the rival families. Whatever had caused the bad blood between the two men, it had happened a long time ago. The Prince didn't know what it was, and he didn't care. He just wanted an end to their quarrel.

'You are both wise, powerful men, and you should be ashamed of yourselves,' he told them. 'You have old bones, and you should know better.'

'They're always picking a fight!' Old Montague muttered angrily.

'The Montagues started it!' Old Capulet quivered, red in the face with rage.

'Liar!' bawled Old Montague. 'You and your whole rotten ...'

'Don't you call me names!' roared Old Capulet.

'If you won't end this quarrel, I will!' vowed the Prince. 'I'm laying down the law for you now. Live in peace on the streets of Verona ... or you'll answer to me with your lives!'

That was the end of the street fight ... but it wasn't the end of the feud, for the two old men still hated each other.

Lady Montague was furious with her husband.

'You doddering fool!' she exclaimed. 'You've more use for a crutch than a sword at your age!' Then she added, with relief, 'At least Romeo wasn't here.'

'Romeo!' grunted the old man. 'He never is! I don't know what's the matter with that son of ours.'

'I saw him this morning,' Benvolio told his uncle. 'I think he went off to the woods to be by himself.'

'That's all he ever does!' said Old Montague. 'I don't know what's going on in his mind. I can understand when young men fight ... especially with those dirty Capulets! But Romeo just wanders around in a dream.'

'What's gone wrong with my dear son?'
Lady Montague asked anxiously.

'He talks to me sometimes,' Benvolio tried
to reassure her. 'Leave it to me. I'll look after
Romeo and make sure he's all right.'

Benvolio went to look for his dreamy-eyed
cousin ... the one Montague who'd missed out
on the fight ... and kept out of trouble, so far.

BENVOLIO'S PLANS

It was stifling hot on the streets of Verona when
Benvolio found his cousin, wandering about
looking aimless and miserable.

'They've been fighting again,' he told
Romeo. 'You missed it ... as you usually do!'

Romeo wasn't listening. 'I'm in love,' he
sighed. 'I've found the dearest, loveliest,
sweetest, kindest, most wonderful girl there ever
was in the world. My love for her is breaking
my heart.'

'Let me guess,' Benvolio said wearily. 'You
love her ... and she doesn't love you?'

'She doesn't like me at all,' Romeo
admitted. 'At least that's what she says. But I
won't give in. Rosaline is so beautiful, so lovely,
so full of grace and ...'

'Oh ... it's Rosaline, is it?' Benvolio said. 'I suppose she's good looking but ...'

'She won't have me!' Romeo moaned. 'What have I left to live for? My beautiful ...'

He went on and on, and Benvolio got fed up. The sun burned the streets as they walked. Benvolio was sweaty and itchy because of the heat, and fed up with listening to Romeo's woes. But he'd promised that he'd keep Romeo out of trouble.

Plan One, Benvolio thought. *Persuade him to pick someone else.*

'Grow up!' he told Romeo. 'If she won't have you, that's it. The city is full of young girls in their bright summer clothes. Try someone else ... take your pick!'

'I *have* taken my pick,' Romeo said stubbornly. 'How could I love anyone else?'

I don't know, Cousin, Benvolio thought to himself, *but my guess is you will soon. At your age, one girl's much the same as another.*

Still, Romeo was his friend as well as his cousin ... and he had promised to keep Romeo out of trouble.

Plan Two, Benvolio thought. *Let him see her again. She's nothing special. Maybe with luck he'll stop wanting her.*

'Well if it has to be Rosaline ... I know where Rosaline will be tonight!' he told Romeo.

'Where?' Romeo asked.

'There's to be a great ball held at the Capulet house. Your sweet Rosaline is invited. Your father wouldn't let you go there ... and neither would Old Capulet. But we could hang about close to the house. You might see her going in or in the street afterwards ...'

'I'll go to the ball!' Romeo said, blinded with love. 'I'll go in and speak to her there. I must. I have to tell her of my love.'

Benvolio knew that Plan Two was in trouble.

'You can't go into the Capulet house! Tybalt would cut you in two if he found you!' he told his cousin.

'I don't care,' Romeo said. 'What does death matter to me if she won't have me?'

Plan Three, Benvolio thought furiously. *Take a chance. Let him go to the ball. Maybe he'll see someone else that he fancies! The problem is ... I'll have to go too, to keep Romeo out of trouble.*

'There is one thing we could do,' he suggested, hopefully. 'We could go in disguise. Lots of people will be masked. If we take care, no one will recognise us.'

They agreed they would go.

Benvolio was stuck with Plan Three.

He was sweating again, and it wasn't because of the sun.

LOVE AT FIRST SIGHT

That night the Capulets' great house glittered with power and riches and glamour. They'd invited all the important families of Verona, everyone but the Montagues. No Montague ever came to that house. No Montague would ever dare *think* of coming.

'You are all very welcome,' Old Capulet said to his guests. 'Lots of dancing for you young ones now, before we eat. I'm not dancing ...!'

'Dance for us!' someone called out.

'Old men's corns aren't made for dancing!' Old Capulet laughed.

It was a wonderful evening. There was rich wine and fine clothes, and the young people there were the pride of Verona. Girls dressed in beautiful dresses, young men whose eyes flashed at the girls. Romance and beauty filled the night air, and soft music played for the dancing.

'Look at Juliet,' Old Capulet said to his wife. 'The loveliest girl here tonight! And the Prince's cousin, Paris, is here. They'd make a wonderful pair. A marriage like that wouldn't do any harm to the Capulet name!'

He didn't see the two young men who'd slipped in to one side, keeping well to the edge of the crowd so that they wouldn't be seen.

'I don't like this!' Benvolio told Romeo, looking round nervously.

Romeo wasn't listening. He was trying to spot the wonderful, gorgeous, exciting, heart-thrilling Rosaline among all the other young girls. Her eyes, her lips, her beautiful hair ...

'Benvolio! What are you doing here?' someone said, and a hand tapped Benvolio's shoulder.

Benvolio swung round, ready to run if he had to. The speaker lowered his mask, and Benvolio breathed again.

It was his friend Mercutio ... but had anyone else heard?

'Don't speak my name!' Benvolio whispered. 'If Tybalt heard you ...'

'... they'd serve Minced-meat-Montague at the feast!' Mercutio said. He was a handsome young man, with laughing eyes.

'Have you come to waltz with Tybalt?' he asked Benvolio. 'Maybe a quickstep outside would be better!'

'It's love's young dream Romeo!' Benvolio hissed furiously. 'He's come looking for his Rosaline. You know the one? "The most wonderful girl in the world," according to him. You and I know she's a crow ... but he won't be told. I'm only here to keep him out of trouble.'

'Trouble is walking our way right now,' Mercutio said, with a nod of his head to Tybalt, who was coming toward them.

'You don't have to tell me that,' Benvolio said. 'Tell Romeo!'

They found Romeo quickly.

'Tybalt's on the warpath,' Benvolio warned him. 'We'd better go.'

'Not yet,' Romeo said. 'How can I go when I've not spoken to Rosaline?'

'One dance ... and we're off!' Benvolio said, nervously.

'I've not come here to dance,' Romeo said. He moved away through the crowd, looking for sweet Rosaline.

He didn't find her. He found someone else instead ... and suddenly no one else in the world mattered ... there was no one else in the world, no one else with this sweetness and light, with those lips and those sparkling eyes smiling at him ...

From across the room, the most beautiful girl in the world was looking straight at him. Then she smiled. She was smiling for him ... Romeo. She had to be ... he just knew it.

'She's wonderful!' Romeo gasped. 'I never saw true beauty till this night!'

Tybalt heard him and recognised his voice ... the mask that he wore couldn't save Romeo.

'A Montague voice ... in our hall!' Tybalt muttered.

Old Capulet saw trouble brewing, and corns or no corns, Old Capulet could move fast when he had to.

He grabbed Tybalt's arm.

'That's Romeo, Uncle ... a Montague in our house!' Tybalt hissed. 'Let me at him.'

'Not here, not now!' said the old man, dragging Tybalt to one side, away from the crowd on the dance floor. 'That boy is my guest.'

'Romeo? Don't tell me you invited him here?' Tybalt said, wrestling free from the old man's grip. 'Fetch me a sword!'

'You've no need of a sword!' said the old man. 'I've heard men speak well of Romeo. You are right. He shouldn't have come to my house. But I won't have you fight him. You heard the Prince warn us this morning.'

'Prince or no Prince ... I'm not standing for this!' Tybalt swore.

'You can ... and you will,' the old man said. 'This is *my* house. I am *Master* here. He stays here ... and you go! Go now! Obey me! Do what I tell you!'

They glared at each other.

'You coward!' Tybalt said.

White with rage, he stalked out of the room.

Romeo didn't know what had happened, and he didn't care.

He was with *her* ... the most wonderful girl in the world. She was talking and laughing and flirting with him.

Their hands touched ... and he felt her touch as a kiss ... the kiss that would be the first of many. He knew ... and she knew ...

Their hands touched again ... and ...

'Sweetheart! My cherub!' A fat old woman pushed in between them. It was the old nurse who had cared for Juliet when she was a baby ... and still treated her like one. 'Your mother wants you! Quick now ... there's someone very, very special she wants you to meet! I told you he would come. I knew that he would. You lucky girl! Hurry up. Go!'

Juliet knew it had to be Paris, and she knew what her mother and father were planning for her and the Prince's young cousin. The old nurse had spent all day telling her about Paris but now ...

Looking back as she went toward her mother, Juliet smiled at Romeo.

'I see love in her eyes!' Romeo thought. 'She wouldn't look at me like that if she didn't love me!'

Romeo stopped the old nurse.

'Who is that girl?' he asked her.

'Why sir, my Juliet ... her mother's the lady of the house! Whoever weds Juliet will get all Old Capulet's money!' she told him.

'Old Capulet's daughter!' groaned Romeo as the nurse followed Juliet.

'Who is that young man I was standing with?' Juliet asked the nurse, as they walked over to her mother and Paris. 'He did not dance, but his eyes followed me round the room.'

'Romeo,' said the old woman. 'He's a Montague. You don't want to know him.'

'Romeo!' Juliet gasped.

The nurse saw the look of dismay on her face.

'The son of your father's worst enemy!' she warned Juliet. 'But he's nothing to you. The man you must marry is Paris.'

But Paris was too late.

Juliet was already in love.

UNTIL TOMORROW

The dancing was finished, the ball was over. The guests had said their thanks to Old Capulet and gone home.

Juliet stood on the balcony outside her room, looking down on the moonlit orchard. She was thinking of Romeo and how he was a Montague.

'What's in a name …? Romeo is more than his name. A rose would still smell as sweet if it was called something else. I love him so much … if only he wasn't called *Montague*!'

She talked softly to herself, believing that she was alone with her thoughts … but she wasn't.

Romeo had slipped away from his friends and climbed over the orchard wall. He was hiding in the shadows close to the balcony and he heard every word.

She loves me! he thought. *Her words tell me so. Now she can never deny it*. He stepped out of the shadows and called softly to her.

'Romeo!' Juliet answered. 'Is it really you? You should not be here. You're in danger. If my family should find you here … you, a *Montague* … they'd kill you.'

'For your love, I would risk anything, even the anger of our families,' he replied.

'You've heard me say what you should not have heard me say so soon,' Juliet said, blushing. 'I've said I love you. If you love me … say so … and tell me that you mean it.'

'I swear it by the moon!' he told her.

'Don't swear by the moon,' she interrupted. 'The moon comes and goes … is your love like that?'

'What shall I swear by then?' Romeo asked.

'Swear by yourself … and I'll believe you,' she said.

'You are my dear love ...' Romeo began.

'Perhaps this is too soon,' she interrupted, confused, still blushing.

'You've told me that you love me. You can't deny it!' Romeo said. 'We must exchange vows and be married.'

'I could not love you more,' she told him softly. The look in her eyes told him all that he needed to know.

Then they heard the old nurse calling.

'My dove! My love! Time for bed, Cherub!' she called.

'I'm coming, Nurse,' Juliet replied. 'Stay here ... I'll be back in a minute,' she whispered to Romeo.

Romeo stayed where he was in the darkness, his heart overflowing with love. How could this wonderful girl love him ...? It seemed as though all the events of that hot summer night were too sweet to be anything more than a dream.

And then she was back, slipping out on to the balcony again with her robe swirling round her and her eyes glowing with love.

'We must marry soon, or they'll part us,' she told him. 'If your words are true ...'

'Tomorrow. I'll get word to you tomorrow. Send a messenger to me in the morning,' he said softly.

'Goodnight! Goodnight!' she said, glancing
back to see if she'd been overheard by the
nurse. 'Parting is such sweet sorrow. I'll say
goodnight ... until tomorrow.'

And then she was gone, back to the room
and her doting old nurse ... who only wanted to
talk about love and romance and young Paris.

Juliet turned pale at the sound of his name
and fell silent.

'What's wrong, Sweetheart?' asked the
nurse, combing Juliet's long black hair.

55

'Nothing,' Juliet said. She started to weep, and the old nurse consoled her.

'You'll marry just who you want to,' the old woman crooned, stroking Juliet's hair. 'Love is all that matters for someone as young and lovely as you. I was young too ... I know how it feels. Trust me. The one that you want is the one that I want for you.'

And Juliet told her about Romeo.

'I promised I'd help you,' the nurse said, doubtfully. 'But why Romeo? Why not that lovely man Paris? Paris is right for you. I know that he is ...'

'I love Romeo,' Juliet told her. 'I won't marry Paris!'

The old nurse loved *love*. She promised to help Juliet.

A SURPRISED PRIEST

At dawn the next morning, Romeo hurried to Friar Laurence, his old friend and adviser, who could marry them quickly.

Friar Laurence had risen early to gather herbs from his garden, outside the city walls. He was a healer as well as a priest, and he used the potions he made from the herbs to heal the people of Verona. The Friar was wise and gentle, and no one who came to him for help was ever turned away.

'You want to marry Rosaline *today*?' the Friar said, when Romeo told him the news.

'Not Rosaline!' Romeo laughed. 'She doesn't come into this. I don't want to marry Rosaline!'

'You were here crying over *Rosaline* yesterday!'

'Rosaline means nothing to me,' Romeo insisted. 'The girl I want to marry is Juliet.'

'Of all the girls in Verona you ... a *Montague* ... want to marry Old *Capulet's* daughter?' the Friar said, still puzzling it out.

'Why not? I love Juliet!' Romeo said. 'Nothing else matters!'

And he kept on saying it. *I love Juliet. I love Juliet. I love Juliet ...*

In the end, the Friar himself began to think *Why not? If a Montague could marry a Capulet ... it might bring peace to Verona, once the two families got over the shock.*

'If you're really sure that you love Juliet ...'

'I am sure. And I'm sure she loves me too,' Romeo insisted.

'Then you'd better be married, I suppose,' grunted the Friar. 'I hope it brings an end to the feud. But why must you marry so soon? What's the hurry?'

'It has to be now, quickly, before our families find out and stop us. You know what they are like. That's why it has to be this afternoon ... not tomorrow or the day after. If our families find out about us, they won't let us marry.'

'The wise move slowly,' the Friar warned Romeo. 'People who run too fast can stumble.'

But Romeo wouldn't listen.

Reluctantly, the Friar agreed to marry Romeo and Juliet in secret that afternoon. It wasn't the kind of grand showy wedding that their families were used to, but that didn't matter to them. They loved one another, and nothing else counted.

'My family will suspect something if I don't go back to my father tonight,' Juliet told Romeo.

'I'm not scared of your father, or mine,' Romeo told her boldly. 'I'll work something out. Go back to your house. Don't tell anyone that we are married until I find somewhere we can go, where they can't separate us.'

Juliet clung to him, not wanting to part.

'It's our wedding night,' she told Romeo, wistfully. 'I don't want to spend it holding hands with my nurse.'

'I'll be with you tonight,' Romeo promised. 'I'll come to you secretly. I swear that nothing will stop me.'

The old feud didn't matter to him any more. He would find a new life with his beautiful wife.

But for others the feud hadn't died. It still raged in the brain of Juliet's hot-tempered cousin, Tybalt. He was furious with his uncle for not allowing him to fight Romeo.

'Romeo has insulted the name Capulet! He came like a thief in disguise to our house. I will have my revenge!' Tybalt swore.

DEATH ON THE STREETS OF VERONA

The afternoon sun blazed down on the streets. It was so hot that men sweated and swore as they walked, and everyone felt ill at ease and bad-tempered.

Tybalt was worst of all. Full of pride in the name Capulet and lust for revenge, he was ready to fight with anybody. When he saw Mercutio he sneered at him, 'You are friend to that scum Romeo!'

'What if I am?' Mercutio said, standing his ground.

Tybalt put his hand on his sword, threateningly. 'I don't like the company you keep!' he glared at Mercutio.

He'd chosen the wrong man to pick a fight with.

Mercutio reached for his sword.

'Gentleman!' said Benvolio, coming between them. 'This is too public a place. Remember the words of the Prince. If you are caught fighting ...'

That's when Romeo appeared, dreaming of love as he strolled down the street toward his friends.

'I've found you ... you villain!' Tybalt swore, his quarrel with Mercutio swiftly forgotten.

Romeo was confused. How could he draw his sword and fight one Capulet, when he had just given his heart to another?

'Don't call me a villain,' Romeo said awkwardly. 'I have ... I have reason to love you.'

His friends were amazed. Romeo had been insulted by Tybalt ... how could he stand there speaking of love? But if Romeo was too scared to fight ... Mercutio certainly wasn't! If Tybalt wanted a fight, he would have one.

'Face me, you rat-catcher!' he yelled at Tybalt.

Tybalt spun round and faced him, drawing his sword. Their blades gleamed in the sun as they lunged at each other.

'We've got to stop them!' Romeo shouted to Benvolio. 'If the Prince catches them fighting ...'

Romeo and Benvolio both drew their swords and thrust them between the two men, trying to beat down the two flashing swords. But Tybalt was too quick. He thrust angrily, and his sword clashed with Romeo's, sliding under it into Mercutio's body.

Blood came from the wound, and Mercutio fell to the ground as Tybalt fled.

'A curse on both your houses!' Mercutio moaned.

Benvolio tried to help his friend. He made his way into a nearby house, carrying Mercutio. But it was too late ... Mercutio died in his arms.

Romeo stood confused in the street outside the house. He didn't know what to do next ... all his hopes were ruins.

It was the old feud again ... Montague and Capulet. If he'd fought Tybalt, Mercutio wouldn't have died. Now he would be blamed for Mercutio's death by the Prince ...

Before he had time to think, Tybalt came rushing back. He'd killed once. Why should he not kill again? It was Romeo that he'd wanted to fight. He'd found Romeo ... and now he would kill him.

'You filthy Capulet!' Tybalt roared.

'Murderer!' Romeo yelled back. 'I'll kill you, or follow my friend to the grave!'

This time there was no standing back, no thought that he was fighting Juliet's cousin.

They fought and Tybalt fell, killed by the swift thrust of Romeo's sword. Benvolio found his cousin standing over Tybalt's dead body, scarcely believing what he had done.

'You must go at once ... before this news reaches the ears of the Prince,' Benvolio told his friend.

'I am cursed with bad fortune!' Romeo cried, as he fled.

The Prince came, bringing with him the two old men whose feud was the cause of the fight, Old Montague and Old Capulet, and their wives.

'Tybalt started the trouble,' Benvolio told the Prince. 'He killed Mercutio ... then Romeo avenged his friend. Tybalt would have been executed for his crime if you'd caught him.'

'My kinsman, Mercutio, has died because of your quarrel,' the Prince told the old men. 'You'll pay for that with your purses! I believe Benvolio's story ...'

'Benvolio is a Montague!' hissed Old Capulet. 'He would say that!'

The Prince wouldn't listen. 'I'll be merciful toward Romeo,' he said. 'There's been enough death because of your feud. I won't add his death to the list. But he must pay for his crime. I banish Romeo from Verona. If he's found here again, he must die!'

The Prince's men hunted for Romeo but they didn't find him. He had left the walled city to seek Friar Laurence.

'The Prince has shown you mercy,' Friar

Laurence said, trying to console him. 'Don't talk of death! Juliet still loves you, though she weeps for the death of her cousin. She sent her nurse here with a ring as a pledge of her love. She pleads with you to come and console her. Go to her tonight, as you had planned. You dare not stay long, or your life is in danger.'

So, that night, Romeo ventured into the city to be with Juliet. The night passed with the two lovers together ... but they had to part before dawn. Perhaps the trouble would pass. Perhaps they could still find a place where they could be together, far away from Verona.

'Stay true to our love!' Romeo told her.

'I'll always love you,' Juliet said. 'That's all that matters to me!'

As the sun rose, Romeo hurried away from Verona to the city of Mantua, thinking Juliet would be safe with her father.

But Old Capulet had other plans for his daughter ...

SHE'LL WEEP NO MORE

Juliet was alone in her room, when her father and mother brought her their good news.

'She weeps for her murdered cousin Tybalt!'

the nurse told them.

'She'll weep no more!' Old Capulet said. 'She's too young to waste her life weeping. We'll make the sun shine in this place of mourning. Life must go on ... we can't see her suffer like this!'

'You weep for Tybalt,' her father said, smiling at her. 'You weep ... but we bring you good news! You're to marry Paris at once. It will bring you new happiness!'

'I can't,' Juliet tried to argue. 'There has been no time for a courtship.'

'Smile now ... Paris will banish your tears,' they told her.

'The marriage must be put off for a while,' Juliet said. 'I am still too upset.'

'You must live!' the old man told her. 'Paris is a good man. You'll be happy. We know he is the right man for you.'

Juliet faced her father. She was already married ... but she couldn't explain that to him.

'I can't marry Paris,' she said. 'I just can't.'

She kept on saying it, until at last Old Capulet lost his temper.

'You can ... and you will!' he roared at her.

'No I won't!'

'You will ... if I have to drag you to the church, you will!' Old Capulet swore, and he stormed out of the room.

Even the old nurse took her parents' side.

'I'm *married* to Romeo,' Juliet told her. '*They* don't know that ... but *you* do. How can you say that I should marry Paris, when I've given my heart to my husband?'

'Romeo might as well be dead as far as you are concerned,' the nurse argued. 'He murdered your cousin Tybalt!'

'But I love Romeo!' Juliet said, bursting into tears again.

'He is a foul Montague, and he killed your cousin,' the old nurse went on. 'You can't forgive him for that. I know I never can. I cared for Tybalt as a child, just as I cared for you. Now you weep for his killer!'

'Romeo ...!' Juliet wailed.

The nurse didn't give up. 'Paris is kind and gentle. He's an eagle compared to that dishcloth you married. I want only the best for my girl. Believe me, I speak from the heart.'

Juliet felt betrayed. *I can't trust you any more. I love Romeo, and I'm not going to marry anyone else ...* she thought to herself. *But I'm not going to tell you that! I'll tell you what you want to hear ... and I'll make my own plans.*

'You've comforted me *marvellously*,' she sniffed. 'And you're right of course, you always are. Who wouldn't marry such a wonderful man?'

'There now, Sweetheart,' said the nurse, patting her head. 'I knew you'd see sense. It will all turn out well in the end. Imagine how happy you'll be, married to Paris.'

'I've been so bad to my parents,' Juliet told her, choosing her words very carefully to deceive the nurse.

'They'll forgive you. They love you so much ... that's why they've made such a good match for you!' the nurse told her.

'Yes but ... I know what I'll do. I'll go to the priest, Friar Laurence, and confess all my sins, and God will forgive me. Tell them that ... tell them I've gone to seek pardon from God for not obeying them.'

'Friar Laurence is wise,' the old nurse agreed. 'He'll help you!'

Juliet hoped she was right. The old priest was part of her secret. He'd married a Montague to a Capulet, without the two families knowing. If he let her marry again, he'd have to answer to God ... and to the Prince of Verona.

The Friar must find a way to save me from this marriage, she told herself.

THE FRIAR'S PLAN

Juliet came to Friar Laurence in despair, not knowing how he could stop the awful thing that was about to happen to her. He already knew about her father's plans and he had been thinking.

'They can't make me marry Paris,' Juliet wept. 'I won't do it. I'll kill myself first.'

'Be still,' he told her. 'I see hope.'

'What hope can there be?' Juliet sobbed.

'Here's what we will do,' he said. 'I have a potion I will give to you. Go home. Tell them you agree to be married ...'

'I would rather be eaten by bears or bitten by snakes!' Juliet interrupted. 'I'd rather lie in the grave ...'

'So you will ... in a way,' the Friar said patiently. Then he told Juliet what he had planned.

'Tomorrow night, on the eve of your wedding to Paris, you must arrange to sleep in your bedchamber alone. Send the nurse away. When you are alone, take this potion. You will fall into a deep sleep. When they find you in the morning, it will seem that you are dead. There will be no sign of breathing, even if they hold a mirror to your lips. Your pulse will be still. They will believe you have died of grief over Tybalt. They will take you and place you in the family vault, as is the custom in this country. You will waken in forty-two hours, and I will be there, with Romeo. I will bring him to you. Then the two of you can escape to Mantua.'

'If I should wake before Romeo comes ...' she said, with a shiver, 'I'd lie alone in the vault with all the dead Capulets.'

'You won't. I will send a message to Romeo. He will be there,' the Friar reassured her.

He gave her the potion, and Juliet returned to her father's house, to make ready for her wedding.

'The Friar has told me to apologise to you for my disobedience,' she told her father.

'The Friar is a good man!' her father

beamed. He started making arrangements for the wedding. It would be a great occasion. He was full of his ambition for Juliet. The name Capulet would be even more important in Verona than before, with his daughter married to the Prince's kinsman.

There was so much to do, and so little time to do it in. All the next day passed with Old Capulet making the arrangements. The church had to be prepared, the guests invited ... and there was Juliet's dress to consider.

Juliet kept her real feelings to herself, hiding them from her mother and the nurse. It was all for a wedding that she knew would never take place, but they must not know that.

At last, all the preparations were finished.

'Let me spend this last night alone in my room,' she told the nurse. '*You* know what I am doing is wrong. I need heaven to smile on it!'

'There's still so much to be done,' the nurse fussed. 'Your lovely dress ... all these wonderful things you will wear for your marriage!'

'Then go to my mother and do it!' Juliet told the old woman.

At last she was alone ... and her fears came to the surface. *If it's poison ... I will die, and the Friar will have found a way to hide the fact that he secretly married us*, she thought to herself, holding the potion.

She would lie with the murdered Tybalt and her ancestors in the vault, among their rotting bones ... and no one would ever know of her secret marriage, and the part that the Friar had played.

'I trust Friar Laurence,' she told herself, with a shiver. 'He's told me the truth. I *will* wake ... and Romeo will be there in the vault beside me when I do.'

Juliet drank the potion. Then she lay down on her bed and waited to die ...

... or to live.

The next morning the nurse hurried to prepare Juliet for her wedding, and found her dead ... at least she seemed dead.

Full of sorrow, the Capulets brought Juliet to the church where she was to have been married and laid her in the family vault.

'With my child, my hopes are buried!' Old Capulet wept, as they sealed the door of the vault.

'It's worked just as I hoped!' thought the Friar. Next he had to make sure that Romeo came to the vault before Juliet wakened. He sent a message to Romeo explaining his plan, but his messenger was delayed. The only message that reached Romeo was the news that Juliet was dead.

'I must go to her,' he cried in despair.

Wild with grief, Romeo returned to Verona. He planned to drink some poison and die there beside his beloved Juliet.

It was night before Romeo reached Verona. He'd come prepared to break the lock and get into the vault. He entered the gloomy graveyard and found his way to the door of the vault where Juliet lay.

'I'll lie beside her tonight!' Romeo vowed, thinking he was alone.

And then someone stepped from the shadows, someone who had drawn his sword.

THE DEATH OF LOVE

Paris had come to Juliet's tomb to weep and to pray for the soul of the girl he'd been going to marry. He was wild with rage when he saw Romeo breaking into the vault.

'What's this? A Montague breaking into the Capulet tomb?' he yelled. 'You'll die for this, Romeo!'

Romeo didn't know who it was who had spoken, but he saw the glint of the sword and he drew his own weapon. They fought, and Paris died swiftly, pierced through the heart by Romeo's sword.

'Lay me with Juliet!' Paris begged with his last breath.

'There's been too much death!' Romeo said sadly, and he dragged Paris' body into the vault.

He found Juliet lying there, and he kissed her. 'With her kiss I die!' Romeo sighed.

He drank the poison he'd brought, so that he could die with her.

Friar Laurence came to the churchyard to be with Juliet when she woke. He found Romeo's body, beside Juliet. As he took in the terrible scene, Juliet stirred.

'Where is Romeo?' Juliet asked.

'Juliet ...' the Friar began.

'Why isn't he here? You promised me Romeo would be here when I woke!' she said.

'Death has been here,' the Friar said, and he showed her Romeo's body.

Juliet was silent. She looked at Romeo lying there.

'Come, Juliet!' the Friar urged. 'We must go. I can hear people coming. I'll hide you away in the convent. No one will know what has happened to you. I swear you'll be safe.'

'I'm not going,' Juliet said. 'Leave me here with my love.'

Fearful of the part he had played in the tragedy, Friar Laurence slipped away.

Alone in the dark tomb, Juliet cradled Romeo's body in her arms, her face against his.

'Your lips are still warm,' Juliet whispered, stroking his hair as she kissed him. 'Romeo … Romeo.' Her fingers closed around Romeo's dagger. 'Let me die!' Juliet sighed, stabbing herself.

They were found in the tomb lying beside each other, together in death.

So it was in Verona, one hot summer a long time ago. Two young lovers died, and two old men wept together for the evil their anger had caused. The deaths of their children had ended the feud … but it was too late to save the young lovers.

HAMLET

A GHOST WALKS

Denmark had won a long war with Norway, but neither side trusted the other. The Danes feared war would soon come again, and there were rumours that a ghost dressed in armour walked in Elsinore Castle.

'Though its face is hidden by a visor, it seems like your father, the King who died two months ago!' Hamlet, Prince of Denmark, was told by his trusted friend Horatio.

That night the Prince and Horatio climbed the stone steps to the broad walk that led round the battlements of the castle. The drunken sounds from the Great Hall followed them.

'The name of Denmark is shamed by those drunken men and their singing!' Hamlet glowered. It seemed no one mourned for the death of his father, not even Queen Gertrude, his mother. Within weeks of her husband's death she had shocked Hamlet by marrying his Uncle Claudius. Now Claudius sat on the throne that had once belonged to Hamlet's father.

Black night hung around them as they emerged on the battlements, the darkness broken only by the flickering glow of torches that lit the guard tower. The wind off the sea was cold. They wrapped their cloaks around them as they waited.

Then the midnight bell rang and something moved in the darkness.

'It comes, My Lord!' Horatio whispered in horror.

The majestic vision came toward them, in full armour, bristling with terrible rage.

'God have mercy!' Horatio moaned, filled with fear.

'Angels defend us!' Hamlet shuddered.

The thing raised an arm, beckoning Hamlet to follow.

'Don't go, My Lord!' Horatio whispered. 'It could be an evil spirit.' He tried to draw Hamlet back, but the young Prince broke away from his friend.

The sound of the wind and the noise of the drunken singing below seemed to fade as Hamlet followed the Ghost along the battlements. Then the Ghost turned to him.

The visor rose … and Hamlet gazed into the tear-filled eyes of his dead father.

The Ghost spoke. 'Mark these words, my son,' it said. 'My time is short. Hell calls me and I must go back there to pay for the sins I committed on earth.'

'I pity you, poor Father,' groaned Hamlet.

'If you love me … you will revenge my murder!' said the Ghost.

'Murder!' Hamlet said, horrified. 'What murder?'

'The serpent who secretly murdered me now wears my crown!' the Ghost said.

'My Uncle Claudius!' gasped Hamlet in horror.

'Your Uncle Claudius poisoned me, and stole my throne. Now he has married my wife … if you are a *man*, you will seek revenge!'

If I am a man Hamlet thought. He knew he wasn't a warrior like his father.

'My mother has betrayed you!' he burst out.

'I loved her so much,' the Ghost said. 'Do nothing to hurt your poor mother. I go now … but remember me, Hamlet! I will be revenged!'

The words roared in Hamlet's head.

Remember me! I will be revenged!

Then the Ghost was gone.

If I am a man Hamlet thought again, and he shuddered. 'That smiling villain! My uncle! The King of Denmark!' He was still muttering blood-curdling words when Horatio reached him.

'Did it speak, My Lord?' the anxious Horatio asked.

'This is my business alone,' Hamlet said, thinking carefully. 'Don't be offended, my friend! What happened here tonight must stay secret. You must promise me. Lay your hands on my sword, and swear that you'll tell no one anything you have seen or heard tonight.'

Horatio swore on his sword, but he still tried to persuade Hamlet to tell him what had happened.

'There are more things in heaven and earth than you dream of Horatio!' was all Hamlet would say. 'Whatever I do after this, however strange I may seem … you must say nothing!'

There was something rotten in the State of Denmark … and Hamlet knew it was up to him to set it right!

My Father will have his revenge.

A TROUBLED MIND

Hamlet wandered the halls of the castle, dressed all in black. The awful words of the Ghost haunted him.

Remember me … I will be revenged.

He was a pale shadow of the lively young Prince he had been, talking to himself, muttering wildly of death and betrayal.

'I know that the Prince says he loves you, but you must stay away from him!' Ophelia, the young girl Hamlet loved, had been ordered by her father Polonius.

'Avoid Hamlet ... he can never marry you,' her brother Laertes agreed.

Ophelia still loved Hamlet ... but she obeyed them. Hamlet saw her sudden coldness toward him as yet another betrayal.

Women are all the same, Hamlet thought. *A woman's beauty is only a trap for men. Ophelia has betrayed me, just as my mother has betrayed my father. How could I expect anything else from a woman?*

Hamlet sought out Ophelia in her chamber, but he was so overcome by his emotions that he could not speak. He took her by the arm and held her, staring hard into her face. Then he turned away from her, and ran from the room.

Scared by what was happening to Hamlet, Ophelia went to her father, Polonius, who was the King's Chief Counsellor.

'I obeyed you, Father,' Ophelia wept. 'I stopped talking to him as you told me to, though I loved him and I still do. The Prince is acting as if he's gone mad. I saw the wild look on his face. There's no knowing what he might do in this strange mood. He frightens me.'

'Perhaps he really *does* love you ... and losing you has driven him mad!' Polonius said, thinking quickly. The old Counsellor saw the danger to his own position.

Hamlet could never marry Ophelia – Polonius was convinced of that. The Prince would make a royal marriage ... he would not marry a Counsellor's daughter. But if Hamlet's love for Ophelia drove the Prince mad, the King might turn against Polonius.

'The King must know of this!' he told her.
'He must be convinced that you did not
encourage the Prince in any way. You must not
be blamed for Hamlet's madness.'

The King and Queen were together in the
Great Hall of the castle and they were talking
about Hamlet. They were both worried about
him ... but for different reasons. Gertrude
loved her son and wanted him to be happy but
Claudius feared the son of the man he had
murdered.

Suppose Hamlet had somehow discovered
the truth about his father's death and the
poison? It was a fear that Claudius couldn't
share with the Queen. She knew nothing of
what he had done to win the throne.

'Hamlet grieves for his father ... and he
dislikes our marriage,' the Queen told her
husband. 'That is what disturbs his mind.'

'I suppose that *could* be it,' Claudius said. 'I
brought his friends here to see if they could find
out what troubles him ... but he suspects that I'm
using them to spy on him and he's told them
nothing. Now the travelling actors he used to
love are coming. Perhaps that will help him.'

'I hope so,' said the Queen. 'He's taking his
grief for his father too far!'

Then Polonius came bustling in with his
story.

'It's not grief for his father that troubles the poor Prince,' he told the King. 'It is his love for my daughter, Ophelia, that makes him act so strangely. She has refused him. Yet he still sends her letters and follows her. The change she sees in him has frightened her.'

Then he stopped talking.

Hamlet had appeared, wandering listlessly, with his head in a book. He was dressed as though he didn't mind what clothes he wore, or what he looked like. He crossed and re-crossed the echoing flagstones of the hall with no thought for anything but the words in his book.

'If it pleases your Majesty, leave him to me,' Polonius whispered to the King, moving toward the young man.

'Do you know me, My Lord?' Polonius asked.

'Well sir, you are a fishmonger,' Hamlet replied, and he tapped his nose, as though he smelt something fishy.

'Not I, My Lord!' gasped the King's Counsellor, taken aback.

'Then I wish you were so *honest* a man,' Hamlet said. 'Tell me, Fishmonger, have you a daughter?'

'Yes, My Lord,' Polonius stammered.

'Take care of her!' Hamlet warned him. 'Who knows what could happen to her? See to it, Fishmonger!' Hamlet seemed to talk in riddles. But were they just riddles? Polonius didn't know.

'There's method in his madness,' the old man thought to himself.

Polonius' way was to scheme and to plan. He had risen to his position of power in Denmark by his plotting, and he meant to keep power that way.

'It's a broken heart that troubles the Prince, Your Majesty,' he told Claudius. 'I'll bring Ophelia and Hamlet together, somewhere where we can overhear what they say ... I'll arrange it so that Hamlet won't know that we're listening. Then you'll know that what I am saying is true.'

'Let it be so,' said the King, keeping his own thoughts to himself.

If Polonius was wrong ... Hamlet would have to be dealt with.

Claudius was ruthless and cunning. He wasn't going to let anyone stand in his way ... certainly not the young Prince.

Hamlet paced the cold corridors of the castle, alone with his thoughts and his conscience. He had to be sure that Claudius had killed his father.

The devil is cunning, he thought. *Suppose he has used a ghost in my father's shape to mislead me? The devil could be using my anger against Claudius and my mother for his own evil ends.*

If the Ghost had told the truth ... Hamlet must kill Claudius.

I am the wrong man for this, Hamlet thought bitterly, still tortured by his doubts and the confusion that clouded his mind.

Somehow, he had to discover the truth ... but how could he do it?

Hamlet found his opportunity with the arrival of the play actors. In happier days he had joked and laughed with them. Now, he would use his friends and the play they were to perform as a way of testing whether the King was innocent ... or guilty.

He sought out Horatio, the only man he could trust. He had told his friend of his terrible suspicions about Claudius. Now it was time to do something.

'The King hopes to cheer me with these actors,' he told Horatio. 'What play are they going to stage?'

'It's called *The Mousetrap*, My Lord,' Horatio told him, pleased to see Hamlet interested in something normal again, even if it were only strolling players and their play.

'Perhaps we can change that,' Hamlet mused. 'I know another play that suits my purpose better, called *The Murder of Gonzago*. It tells of the death of a Duke. I'll make changes in it, just for this one performance. The actors have been my friends for a long time. If I ask them, they'll do what I say. But I need you to do something for me.'

'Of course, My Lord,' said his friend.

'Watch the King carefully during the play,' Hamlet said. 'Tell me what you see in his face! The play's the thing! It will show us if he's guilty.'

Hamlet's trap was set.

TO BE OR NOT TO BE

Ophelia was alone in the Great Hall, reading a book. Her father had told the frightened girl that she was to appear loving and friendly toward the mad Prince. Hamlet scared her with his look of madness and anger as he stalked silently through the castle ... but she still loved the man she was about to betray.

Hamlet came, pacing the hall, deep in his own thoughts, muttering, his mind dark with gloom and fear of what he might have to do ... if he could bring himself to do it.

The King and Polonius were concealed in a curtained alcove, and they heard his footsteps echo on the stone floor as he approached their hiding place.

'To be ... or not to be?' Hamlet mused. The

words he spoke were only for himself. 'To live ... or to die?'

He was filled with indecision, distracted by his own doubts, his grief and anger and his indecision.

He could live, take up arms, fight against his troubles ... and end them ... or choose to die.

To die would be an easier choice. He could slip into the sleep of death, the world of dreams, the unknown world that lay beyond the grave ... but it was a world he feared. Who knew what was there?

Then he realised that he was not alone.

'Ophelia!' he breathed.

Her pale face was rouged, her soft hair flowed around her and she was the picture of innocence as she turned toward him ... but he saw no innocence there.

'How are you, My Lord?' she asked, with her eyes lowered.

'I'm well!' he said impatiently. He didn't want to talk to her now and was looking for a way to escape.

'You loved me once, or so you said,' she told him.

'No, not I!' he said.

'You know you did!' she answered.

'If I said I loved you once, I lied,' he told her. 'You should not have believed me.'

'You deceived me,' she accused him.

'Go to a nunnery ... or marry a fool who will trust you!' he told her cruelly.

'You're sick!' she told him. 'You must be sick to speak this way to me.'

'Take that paint off your face. God gave you one face and you make it another,' he went on cruelly. 'Women are all the same. Wise men never marry ...'

'Sweet heavens!' Ophelia gasped.

'I'll say no more of marriage,' Hamlet muttered, speaking almost to himself as he turned away from the weeping Ophelia and left the Great Hall. 'Those that are married already, all but one, shall live.'

All but one.

Claudius heard the words. To the ruthless King, *all but one* could mean only one thing. Hamlet had discovered the truth. The words the Prince had spoken sealed his fate.

'It's not love that's troubling the Prince,' Claudius told Polonius sharply, as they came out from the alcove where they had been hiding. 'He needs a change of scene, somewhere different. I'll send him to the King of England for a while, to collect our taxes, and we'll have peace.'

'That's a good thought, Your Majesty,' said Polonius, 'yet I'm still sure that it is his love for Ophelia that is the cause of his strange behaviour. Why don't you ask his mother to talk to him after the play tonight and see if she can get the truth from him?'

If Hamlet tells Gertrude the truth ... that I murdered his father ... Claudius thought guiltily.

Polonius saw doubt and fear in the King's face, but he still didn't suspect the real reason behind it. He was anxious to prove that his own idea was right.

'The Queen loves Hamlet so much that he might say something to her that he won't say to you,' Polonius said persuasively. 'With your permission, I'll listen to their talk and I will tell you everything that he says. Then you'll know if sending him to England is the best thing to do.'

Claudius agreed, but his mind was already made up. Hamlet would go to England ... and he would never return. Claudius would arrange it with the English King.

The Prince would be put to death on some trumped-up charge, or be found murdered, or simply disappear. *How* Hamlet lost his life didn't matter to Claudius. All that mattered was that the King of Denmark should not be blamed for his death.

Claudius had killed once for the throne. One more death ... and he would be safe.

Whatever Hamlet knew of the King's guilt would die with him.

THE PLAY'S THE THING

It was time for the play ... Hamlet's trap.

The Great Hall was full of activity and chatter, as the strolling players set up their stage and studied the new words Hamlet had written for their play. It meant more work for them ... but they were excited as they studied their new lines. It was a great honour for them to play at the King's castle, and now the crowd had gathered. All the nobles of Denmark ... and their King.

As Claudius took his place the chattering of the audience died away and the Hall fell silent.

The King watched as the play began ... but his mind was elsewhere, brooding on the fate he had planned for Hamlet, and how he would bring it about.

His thoughts were elsewhere, but then what was happening on the stage drew his mind back to the play.

An old man, a Duke, Gonzago ... sleeping in a garden, while others plotted round him.

Suddenly Claudius was paying attention.

An old man ... a garden.

The King's back stiffened. He looked swiftly round him. It seemed to him that all the audience were intent on the play ... everyone but Horatio, Hamlet's friend.

Horatio's eyes were fixed on the King.

Poison ... there was talk of poison.

Claudius' throat went dry with fear. He half rose from his throne, then pulled himself back.

Poison slipped in the Duke's ear ...

'Next, the poisoner will marry the dead Duke's wife,' Hamlet murmured.

But Claudius couldn't let it happen.

'Stop the play!' he roared, losing all control of himself as he rose in anger, bawling for the lights to be raised.

The King stalked angrily from the room, scattering the audience and cursing, his face red with fury. The bewildered audience quickly followed their King, and the unhappy players were bundled off the stage by the King's servants and sent on their way in disgrace.

Hamlet and Horatio were left alone by the deserted stage, where the King's guilt had been made plain for all to see. The audience would talk, and wonder at the cause of the King's fierce reaction to the play.

'You saw the King's face?' Hamlet asked.

'I saw him!' Horatio replied.

'We got as far as the poisoning ... he knew what was to come!' Hamlet said. 'The story the Ghost told me is true. Claudius poisoned my father, the King.'

Remember me ... I will be revenged. The words filled his brain. He knew now that he had no alternative. He must kill Claudius ... but first he had to go to his mother's room as she had asked him to.

Do nothing to hurt her. Leave Gertrude to heaven ... those were the Ghost's words. Hamlet would obey the Ghost, but he would make his mother understand the terrible thing she had done.

'I'll use words like daggers to cut her!' he told himself.

Queen Gertrude was pale and angry when Hamlet came to her. She was bewildered by her husband's rage at Hamlet's re-working of the old play and was determined to confront the young Prince with what he had done.

'Hamlet, your father has been very

offended by this ...' she began.

Your father! thought Hamlet. She meant Claudius. Claudius was no father of his.

'You offended *my* father!' he answered bitterly, his eyes blazing at her.

'Don't play with words!' she said angrily.

'You are the Queen. My uncle's wife! How could you marry him? How could you forget my father? How could you do it, Mother!' Hamlet said.

He dragged her roughly to a mirror. Thrusting her face against it, he held her there, confronting her own reflection in the glass.

'Look at your face!' Hamlet hissed in her ear. 'What do you see there?'

'You're hurting me! Help! Help!' the Queen moaned.

The curtain beside the bed stirred ... and Hamlet saw it. Someone was there ... in his mother's room ...

Claudius ... it had to be!

Now Hamlet's hour had come.

'What's this? A rat!' he said, drawing his sword.

He stabbed savagely through the curtain, again and again, feeling his sword thrusting deep into the body it concealed. There was a terrible groan of despair from behind the curtain.

'What bloody deed have you done?'
Gertrude cried.

'As bloody a deed as to kill a King!' snapped
Hamlet, pulling the curtain aside, expecting to
find Claudius dead, and his revenge accomplished.

Polonius' body lay on the floor, against the
curtain which had concealed him.

Hamlet turned back to his mother, fierce in
his anger. He yelled and screamed at her in a
torrent of bitterness, accusing her of all he
believed she had done.

Then, as Hamlet shouted, the Ghost came

again, standing before him as though to protect Gertrude.

'Look at him!' Hamlet told her.

'Look at who?' asked the Queen, who could see no one.

'Do you see no one there? It is my father!' Hamlet said, but the Ghost vanished.

Remember me ... I will be revenged! Hamlet thought. The Ghost had come to spur him on.

'This is madness!' breathed the Queen. Now she knew Hamlet was mad ... and in his madness he had killed Polonius.

'What I have said is not madness,' Hamlet told her. 'I know what I am doing.'

'No more,' she told him tearfully. 'You are cutting my heart in two with your words!'

'Then throw away the evil half!' he snapped.

He dragged Polonius' body from the room ... and Gertrude ran to the King to tell him what had happened and to plead for mercy for her son.

Mercy ... for Hamlet?

The death of Polonius played straight into the hands of the ruthless King, but the weeping Gertrude didn't understand that.

She pleaded desperately for her son's life with a King who'd already decided that Hamlet must die.

'Your son will not die for this,' Claudius said, pretending to console his weeping wife. 'I'll cover up what Hamlet has done and send him to England as I had planned ... but I'll send him at once, before word of this comes out.'

He arranged for Hamlet to be taken from the palace, and put on board ship to sail for England ... and the certain death he had arranged for the Prince.

That was the plan ... but Hamlet saw through it and escaped during the journey. He had only one thing on his mind now. It was decided. There was no room left for doubt any more.

He would return to Elsinore and kill the King.

But another man reached the King first. It was Laertes, Polonius' son, seeking revenge for the death of his father.

THE KING PLOTS AGAIN

The King had ordered Polonius' burial to be kept secret, and conducted without ceremony, but somehow the news crept out to the people. No one knew how the old man had died, or who had killed him, or where ... but they knew he was dead in his grave, and tongues wagged.

'The King's Chief Counsellor, dead and buried by night! His daughter Ophelia gone out of her mind with grief.' The rumours spread quickly.

The death of such a well known man could not have happened without the King knowing about it ... and yet the King had ordered it to be kept a secret. If the King had a hand in his Counsellor's death, what did that make the King?

Filled with rage and pain, Laertes returned to Elsinore to seek out the King. He forced his way through the guards into the castle and confronted Claudius, with his sword drawn.

'What treason is this?' asked the King. He had to speak carefully. He knew that the people were behind Laertes. One false move and they might make Laertes their King in his place.

'My father has been murdered,' Laertes swore angrily. 'You ordered my father to be buried at midnight, in secret, so that no one would know. The facts speak for themselves. You killed him or he died by your orders!'

'Not I,' said Claudius. 'I loved your father.'

'Lying King!' Laertes sneered at him.

'I don't fear you,' said the King, trying to calm him. 'I've done nothing to hurt you.'

'Then how did my father die?' Laertes demanded. 'I must know who killed him!'

'You speak like a loving son,' Claudius said.
'I grieve for Polonius as you do. The man who
killed him also threatens me ... Hamlet is my
enemy too.'

'Hamlet!' gasped Laertes. 'The Prince?'

'Prince Hamlet killed your father,' Claudius
told him firmly ... and for once he was telling
the truth. This time, the truth suited the King.

'Then why has justice not been done?'
demanded Laertes. 'Why has Hamlet not been
brought to trial?'

'Two reasons,' said Claudius. 'The Queen
loves her son and I do not wish to grieve her.
And the people of Denmark love the young
Prince. They would believe any story Hamlet
told them about the night of your father's death.'

At that moment a messenger arrived telling
the King of Hamlet's escape and that he was on
his way back to the castle.

'Hamlet is coming back tomorrow!' the
King told Laertes, seizing his chance. If Laertes
was angry and wanted revenge, then Claudius
could make use of his anger, and play one
dangerous man off against another.

'Good!' said Laertes. 'I'll accuse him in
court if you don't dare to! My father is dead.
My sister walks round the castle singing strange
songs and pulling petals from flowers as though
she had nothing to live for. He's ruined my

family and I'll make him pay for it!'

'Calm down,' Claudius said. 'You shall have justice ... but not in a trial.'

'I'll cut Hamlet's throat!' Laertes burst out furiously.

'Then you'd be called a murderer,' Claudius told him carefully. 'Hamlet's a popular prince. No, it needs to look like an accident so that even the Queen doesn't suspect anything.' And he told Laertes his plan. Laertes was so angry with Hamlet that he agreed.

So Hamlet's death was arranged yet again by his uncle, the King ... but another death came before the Prince returned to the castle. Ophelia was found drowned in a stream with flowers floating around her.

It was said that she'd wandered by a stream, and leant on the branch of a willow, and the branch broke. She fell in the water and the weight of her clothes had caused her to drown.

So it was said ... but many knew of her madness and sorrow, and doubted the words they were told.

'My innocent young sister took her own life from grief over our father's death!' Laertes told himself.

Polonius and Ophelia ... now Laertes had two deaths to avenge. Full of anger, he waited for Hamlet's return.

A PLACE OF SKULLS

Hamlet had returned to seek revenge for his father and the only question now was how and when he would kill Claudius. As he came close to Elsinore, he heard a bell toll from the church that lay outside the castle, beside the graveyard.

A fresh grave had been dug by two gravediggers who were sifting the bones they had dug from the earth. One held a skull he had picked from the grave they were digging, and he showed it to Hamlet.

'Who was this?' Hamlet asked, as he held the skull in his hands, still brooding on what he had come to do.

'Yorick ... your father's jester, My Lord,' said the gravedigger.

'Alas, poor Yorick,' sighed Hamlet. 'I knew him well.'

It set him thinking of death yet again. He had laughed and played with the man whose skull he held in his hand. Now Yorick was dust and forgotten. The whole world seemed a place of death and sadness.

Then the church bell tolled. From the church came a coffin followed by the whole court. The procession was led by a priest and Laertes, and behind him came the King and Queen and the Danish nobles.

Laertes was weeping ... and so was the Queen. They stood by the open grave, as the coffin was lowered.

'We'll keep the service short,' said the Priest. 'We're having more ceremony than we should, for she may have died by her own hand. If it hadn't been for the King's orders, she would have been buried outside the church grounds.'

'My sister will be an angel, when you howl in hell!' Laertes swore at him.

'Ophelia!' gasped Hamlet. 'Ophelia is dead.'

All his love for Ophelia came rushing back, and there were tears in his eyes as he pushed his way through the crowd to the graveside.

'Sweets to the sweet,' the Queen said sadly, tossing flowers into the grave. 'You should have had these flowers when you wed my poor son Hamlet.'

Laertes sobbed with rage at her words. He was filled with grief for his sister and it was all that they could do to stop him leaping down into the grave. And then he saw Hamlet ... the man who had murdered his father Polonius and who'd brought Ophelia to her early grave.

It was too much for Laertes. He forgot all about the King's plan for the death of Hamlet. In a moment the two young men were at each other's throats. Their faces were both stained with tears as they wrestled, with the mud of the grave on their clothes.

'Hamlet! Hamlet!' the Queen pleaded, her heart overflowing with sorrow and fear.

'Separate them!' King Claudius ordered quickly.

The others moved in and dragged the two men apart, both still seething with the rage that came from their grief.

'The devil take you!' Laertes cried, struggling in vain to reach the young Prince.

'I loved Ophelia more than forty thousand

brothers!' Hamlet wept pitifully, in the face of Laertes' anger.

'Hamlet must be mad to say that to you!' Claudius told Laertes, trying to calm the young man.

'Don't harm my son,' the Queen pleaded.

'I'm not your enemy!' Hamlet tried to tell Laertes, but the young man wouldn't listen. He was too angry to hear Hamlet's words.

The King told Horatio to take care of the Prince, and Horatio led the weeping Hamlet away. Hamlet looked back sadly at Ophelia's brother, who still stood with his head bowed, as the King talked to him.

I should have been kinder to Laertes, he thought. *He has lost his father and his sister and he loved them both.*

'Gertrude ... watch over your son,' the King warned the Queen. 'There must be peace, in honour of this grave.' Then he grasped Laertes by the arm and pulled him away from the graveside.

'Remember what we agreed!' Claudius whispered ... and Laertes remembered.

'You will have your revenge!' Claudius consoled him. 'For now ... you must act as though Hamlet was your Prince, and your friend, if you can. Seek his pardon for what you have done. Let him believe it was caused by your grief for Ophelia.'

'I understand,' the young man said, bowing his head.

The crowd turned away. They left the churchyard, talking about the strange scene they had witnessed ... two men who fought at the grave of a young woman ... one man her brother, the other her lover. How the Queen wept, and the strained face of the King ... what did this mean for Denmark?

The coffin lay six feet underground, with the flower petals spread on its lid. Ophelia was dead ... but there would be more deaths in Elsinore before long.

REVENGE!

King Claudius feared Hamlet, and he knew that he had to act quickly, if his plan was to succeed. He didn't waste any time.

'What is this, My Lord?' Horatio asked Hamlet. 'For tonight's entertainment in the Great Hall *you* are to fence with *Laertes*, to settle a bet for the King?'

'The King has bet six horses against six good French swords that Laertes cannot beat me,' Hamlet replied, showing no concern. 'The King wants to show that Laertes and I have made peace with each other. If we meet in a sporting match before the whole court, everyone will believe that our quarrel is over.'

'I don't like this,' Horatio said. 'Laertes is a good swordsman ... you could lose. Don't fight him. I will tell the King that you are not fit for such a match after your journey.'

'I trust Laertes. He will play fair,' Hamlet said confidently. 'And I trust my own swordsmanship against his. Don't worry, Horatio. I can beat him.'

So that evening, before the whole court, Laertes and Hamlet met in the Great Hall to fence with light swords.

'It is as we planned,' the King told Laertes. 'The swords are tipped with buttons to make everyone believe that neither man can be hurt ... all but one sword. Let Hamlet take a sword from the rack ... you know him, he'll just take any one ... but you pick with care. Take the sword with *no* button. It has poison on it ... one scratch on his skin, and Hamlet will die. It will seem accidental, and you won't be blamed.'

'What if I don't manage to scratch him?' asked Laertes.

'You will!' said the King. 'But I've thought of that too. The heat of this room as you fight will make Hamlet thirsty. I'll poison a goblet filled with wine specially for him ... it will be there, if we need it.'

The two young men faced each other.

'Do you forgive me our quarrel, Laertes?' Hamlet asked. Laertes smiled, and took a firmer grip on his weapon.

They saluted each other with their swords, and the fight started. It was a swift and skilful duel. They moved light-footed around the hall. One would lunge with his sword, the other would parry. Lunge, parry, lunge ... it went on, fast and furious. Each move met with applause, for both men were showing great skill.

Hamlet scored the first hit, and the fight stopped.

'I drink to your success, Hamlet!' said the King. He raised the goblet of wine to his lips and drank from it. He wanted everyone to see he had drunk from the goblet. That was important. No one could claim that he had poisoned the wine, if he'd drunk the same wine himself.

As all eyes turned back to the two men, Claudius slipped the poison into the goblet.

'Will you drink, Hamlet?' he called, holding the goblet out to Hamlet. 'You must be thirsty.'

'Not yet, My Lord! Later,' Hamlet said.

Claudius put the goblet back on the table.

The two men fought the next round fiercely, and Hamlet scored another hit. He was still untouched by Laertes' poisoned sword.

'Well done, my son!' the Queen said, wiping Hamlet's brow. 'A toast to my son's swordsmanship!' and before Claudius could stop her ... she lifted the goblet and drank.

Claudius sank back in his chair, his eyes cold as stone. He knew there was nothing he could do that would save her, for the poison was deadly and fast.

The two men were fighting again. Swift-footed, they moved round the floor. Then a thrust from Laertes' sword touched Hamlet's leg, lightly. A thin trickle of blood spread from the scratch on his leg.

They fought on. The two swords fell to the floor as they struggled ... and Hamlet picked up Laertes' sword.

The fight continued and then Laertes was cut by a flashing stroke from the poisoned sword.

Both men stood bleeding ... and then the Queen seemed to faint at the sight of their blood.

Hamlet ran to her.

'I'm poisoned! It was the wine from the goblet ...' she moaned, as she died.

'Who did this?' Hamlet whispered. 'Who killed my mother?'

Laertes stood dripping blood from his own wound. Already he could feel the effects of the poison. He fell to the floor, dying.

'Look no further than the King, Hamlet!' he groaned, as he lay dying. 'The sword that wounded us both was tipped with poison. We're both dying and nothing can save us.'

Remember me ... I will be revenged.

The words throbbed in Hamlet's mind as the poison worked through his body. Gasping with pain, his strength ebbing away, Hamlet thrust the poisoned sword through the King's body. Then he lifted the goblet.

'Die like my mother!' Hamlet said, and he poured the rest of the poisoned wine down Claudius' throat.

Horatio held his friend as he died. 'Goodnight, sweet Prince,' he said softly.

That night the bodies of King Claudius and his Queen and Hamlet lay in state in the Great Hall, but no Ghost walked on Elsinore's walls.

Hamlet's father had had his revenge.